HEINEMANN GUIDED R

BEGINNER LEVEL

SO-CAF-002

GEORGE ELIOT

The Mill on the Floss

Retold by Florence Bell

HEINEMANN

BEGINNER LEVEL

Series Editor: John Milne

The Heinemann Guided Readers provide a choice of enjoyable reading material for learners of English. The series is published at five levels – Starter, Beginner, Elementary, Intermediate and Upper. At **Beginner Level**, the control of content and language has the following main features:

Information Control

The stories are written in a fluent and pleasing style with straightforward plots and a restricted number of main characters. The cultural background is made explicit through both words and illustrations. Information which is vital to the story is clearly presented and repeated where necessary.

Structure Control

Special care is taken with sentence length. Most sentences contain only one clause, though compound sentences are used occasionally with the clauses joined by the conjunctions 'and', 'but', and 'or'. The use of these compound sentences gives the text balance and rhythm. The use of Past Simple and Past Continuous Tenses is permitted since these are the basic tenses used in narration and students must become familiar with these as they continue to extend and develop their reading ability.

Vocabulary Control

At **Beginner Level** there is a controlled vocabulary of approximately 600 basic words, so that students with a basic knowledge of English will be able to read with understanding and enjoyment. Help is also given in the form of vivid illustrations which are closely related to the text.

For further information on the full selection of Readers at all five levels in the series, please refer to the Heinemann Readers catalogue.

Contents

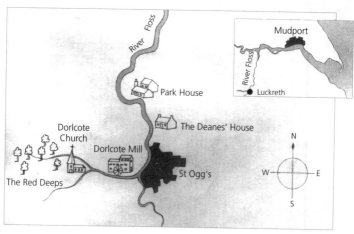

A Note About the Author

George Eliot was born in Warwickshire, England on 22nd November 1819. 'George Eliot' was the name of the writer, Mary Ann Evans. In the 1800s, not many women's books were published. So Mary Ann wrote books with the name, George Eliot.

Mary Ann's father, Robert, worked on an estate – a large amount of land belonging to a rich man. Robert Evans was the estate manager. His three children, Mary Ann, Isaac and Chrissy went to good schools. They were well educated.

Mary Ann Evans was not pretty. But she was very intelligent. Mary Ann learnt French, German, Italian, Greek and Latin. She studied English literature, music, philosophy and religion.

Mary Ann's mother died in 1836 and her father died in 1846. So Mary Ann went to live in London. In London, she was called Marian and she wrote books and magazine articles.

Marian had many friends. They were poets, writers and scientists. Some of her friends were Ralph Waldo Emerson, Charles Dickens, Henry James, W.M. Thackeray, Lord Alfred Tennyson and Charles Darwin.

In 1854, Marian met George Henry Lewes. He was an actor and a writer. Marian and George loved each other. But they did not get married.

George had a wife and he had four children. George and Marian lived together for 23 years. They were not accepted by society. For many years, nobody invited them to their homes. George and Marian were not invited to parties. People did not speak to them. George Lewes died in November 1878, and Marian was very unhappy. She married a good friend, John Cross, in 1880. She died on 22nd December 1880.

George Eliot wrote *Adam Bede* (1859), *The Mill on the Floss* (1860), *Silas Marner* (1861), *Daniel Deronda* (1876), *Romola* (1863) and *Middlemarch* (1872).

A Note About This Story

Time: 1828–1840. **Place**: The east of England.

Maggie Tulliver lives at Dorlcote Mill, near the River Floss. Maggie's father is Edward Tulliver. He is a miller. Farmers bring their corn to the mill. Tulliver makes their corn into flour. Dorlcote Mill is next to a small river. The water from the river runs over a huge wheel. And the wheel turns round. Two huge mill stones also turn round. The corn is put between the two huge stones. The stones turn and the corn is ground into flour for bread.

The land around Dorlcote Mill is flat and there are many rivers. Lots of rain makes the water in the rivers deep and dangerous. In this story, a very great amount of rain falls. The water rises up and out of the rivers. Then there is flooding. The water covers the fields and houses. The rushing water pulls down trees and buildings.

carriage

Note: St = Saint (e.g. St Ogg's).

The People in This Story

Edward Tulliver
'edwəd 'tʌlɪvə

Bessy Tulliver
'besɪ 'tʌlɪvə

Tom Tulliver
'tɒm 'tʌlɪvə

Maggie Tulliver
'mægɪ 'tʌlɪvə

Mrs Glegg
'mɪsɪz gleg

Mr Glegg
'mɪstə gleg

Mrs Deane
'mɪsɪz diːn

Mr Deane
'mɪstə diːn

Lucy Deane
'luːsɪ diːn

Stephen Guest
'stiːvən gest

Lawyer Wakem
'lɔɪjə 'weɪkəmə

Philip Wakem
'fɪlɪp 'weɪkəm

7

1

Brother and Sister

Dorlcote Mill was on the River Floss. The mill was a mile from the town of St Ogg's.

Edward Tulliver was the miller. He lived in the house next to the mill. The miller and his wife, Bessy Tulliver, had two children – a boy, Tom, and a girl, Maggie. Tom was eleven years old. Maggie was nine years old.

It was an afternoon in March 1828. Mrs Tulliver and Maggie were standing outside the house. They were waiting for Mr Tulliver and Tom. Tom had been away at school. He was coming back for the holidays.

'Here is the horse and cart!' Maggie shouted. 'Here is Father. Tom is with him. Tom is back from school!'

'Hello, Mother. Hello, Maggie,' said Tom.

'Oh, Tom, I'm happy to see you,' Maggie said.

'I'm happy to see you, Maggie,' Tom replied. 'I'm going to see my rabbits now.'

Maggie cried out. Her face was white. 'I've got some money, Tom,' she said. 'Buy some more rabbits.'

'More rabbits? I don't want any more rabbits.'

'Oh, Tom!' said Maggie. 'Your rabbits are all dead!'

Tom looked at Maggie. His blue eyes were angry.

'You didn't feed my rabbits, Maggie! You forgot?' Tom shouted. 'I hate you, Maggie! You are cruel!'

Maggie started to cry.

'I'm sorry, Tom,' she said. 'Don't be angry. I'm never angry with you.'

'I never do anything wrong,' said Tom. And he walked away into the garden.

Maggie ran into the house. Tom did not love her! She cried and cried.

Later, Tom came into the house. Mr and Mrs Tulliver were eating cake and drinking tea.

'Where is Maggie?' Mr Tulliver asked.

'I don't know,' said Tom.

'You must take care of your sister,' said Mrs Tulliver.

'Maggie came into the house,' Tom said. 'She was crying.' He took a big piece of cake. He sat down and he started to eat it.

'Crying!' Mr Tulliver shouted. 'Why was she crying? Go and find her!'

Tom went slowly upstairs. He went into Maggie's bedroom. His sister was lying on the bed. She stood up and ran towards him.

'Oh, Tom. I'm sorry about your rabbits,' Maggie said. 'I am a naughty girl.'

'I forgive you, Maggie,' Tom said. 'Stop crying now.'

And Maggie smiled.

2

Maggie Cuts Her Hair

Ten days later, Mrs Tulliver's married sisters came to dinner at Dorlcote Mill. Their husbands, Mr Glegg and Mr Deane, came with them. And Mr and Mrs Deane brought their daughter, Lucy.

Maggie kissed her little cousin. Lucy Deane was seven years old. She had pretty, fair hair. Maggie's hair was dark and untidy.

Everybody sat down at the table.

'Maggie's hair is always untidy,' Mrs Tulliver said. 'What can I do?'

'Cut her hair shorter,' replied Mrs Glegg.

'Go and brush your hair, Maggie,' said Mrs Tulliver. 'Go quickly! We are going to eat dinner now.'

Then Maggie had an idea. She spoke to her brother.

'Come upstairs with me, Tom,' she said quietly.

Maggie and Tom went upstairs. They went into their mother's bedroom. Maggie picked up a pair of scissors.

'What are you going to do, Maggie?' Tom asked.

Maggie cut off a long piece of her hair.

'Oh, Maggie! You are a naughty girl!' Tom said.

Maggie cut off some more hair. Then she gave the scissors to Tom. 'Help me, Tom. Quickly!' she said.

Tom cut once, twice, three times. Soon, pieces of Maggie's hair covered the floor.

Tom looked at his sister and he laughed.

'Don't laugh at me, Tom,' said Maggie.

'Everybody will laugh at you,' Tom said. 'I'm going downstairs now.'

Maggie looked in a mirror. She saw her short hair. She started to cry.

Ten minutes later, Maggie went downstairs. She walked quietly into the dining-room. She sat down.

Mrs Tulliver saw her daughter. She screamed and dropped a plate. Everybody looked at Maggie.

'Who is this?' said Mr Deane. He laughed.

'Maggie is a naughty girl,' said Mrs Glegg.

Maggie started to cry again. She stood up and she ran to her father.

'Don't cry, Maggie,' Mr Tulliver said. 'I love you. I will take care of you.'

———

After dinner, Tom, Maggie and Lucy went into the garden. Mr and Mrs Tulliver talked to the Deanes and the Gleggs.

'Mr Tulliver,' said Mrs Tulliver, 'tell everybody your plan.'

'I want Tom to have a good education,' Mr Tulliver said. 'He will go to a new teacher in August. He will go to Mr Stelling. He will learn everything – history, Latin, mathematics—'

'Tom doesn't need Latin,' Mrs Glegg said. 'He is going to be a miller.'

'He is not going to be a miller,' Mr Tulliver replied. 'He's not as clever as Maggie. But I want Tom to have a good education.'

'Tom must learn useful things, not Latin.' Mrs Glegg said. 'That is my advice.'

Mr Tulliver did not like Mrs Glegg. 'You always give advice,' he said. 'But you don't give people money.'

'No. I don't give people my money,' Mrs Glegg replied. 'But I have lent my money. I have lent money to somebody in this room!'

Mr Tulliver was very angry.

'Yes!' he shouted. 'You have lent me five hundred pounds! And I pay you interest! I pay you twenty-five pounds every year!'

'Don't shout at me!' said Mrs Glegg. Then she stood up. 'Mr Glegg, take me home,' she said.

'Yes! Go home, Mrs Glegg!' Mr Tulliver shouted. 'I will pay you the money next week!'

Mrs Glegg left the room and her husband followed her.

But Mr Tulliver did not have five hundred pounds. He could not pay Mrs Glegg. The next week, he went to a friend. He borrowed the money. He borrowed five hundred pounds. Then he paid Mrs Glegg.

3

Mr Stelling's School

In August 1828, Tom went to live at Mr Stelling's school. Tom was lonely and unhappy. The work was very difficult.

The school was at King's Lorton. It was many miles from St Ogg's. Tom did not go back to Dorlcote Mill until December.

Tom went back to the mill for the Christmas holiday. He spoke to his father.

'Why must I learn Latin?' Tom asked. 'I hate Latin! My Uncle Deane is a rich businessman. He did not learn Latin.'

'You must learn Latin, Tom,' Mr Tulliver said. 'Then you can learn about the law. Our neighbour wants to take water from the River Floss. He wants the water for his land. But I need the water for the mill.'

'There will be a law suit,' Mr Tulliver said. 'Our neighbour is wrong. We will fight our neighbour in the law court. You must learn about the law, Tom. Then you can help me in the law court.'

'Lawyer Wakem will speak for our neighbour,' Mr Tulliver said. 'He will speak in the law court. Wakem is a very bad man. I hate him!'

'Mr Wakem's son, Philip, will go to Mr Stelling's school,' said Tom. 'He is going to study with Mr Stelling too. He will be at the school after Christmas.'

'Philip Wakem is a thin, weak boy,' Mr Tulliver said. 'He is clever. But you are as clever as him.'

So, after Christmas, Tom went back to Mr Stelling's school. When Tom arrived, a boy with a sad face was standing in the library. The boy was thin and he had a twisted back. He was two years older than Tom.

'Hello,' said the boy. 'I'm Philip Wakem.'

'I'm Tom Tulliver,' Tom replied.

4

Philip Wakem

In 1830, Tom Tulliver was thirteen years old. He had been living at Mr Stelling's school for two years. Every day, he had to study for many hours.

Tom was not clever. The work was difficult for him. Philip Wakem was very clever. The work was not difficult for him.

Maggie often wrote letters to Tom. Maggie was eleven years old. She was clever. In her letters, she told Tom all the news. She told him about Dorlcote Mill and about the town of St Ogg's. And Tom often wrote letters to Maggie. One day, he wrote

Dear Maggie

I want to see you. Come and visit me. Mr Stelling is a kind man. You can stay for a few days. Please come soon.
Your loving brother Tom

Maggie wrote to Tom. She was going to visit him soon. Tom was very happy.

Two days before Maggie's visit, Tom found an old sword in Mr Stelling's house. The sword was heavy and sharp. Tom was very pleased. 'I will show this sword to Maggie. It will frighten her!' he thought.

It was afternoon. Maggie was staying at Mr Stelling's school. The boys were in the library. They were reading their books.

Maggie sat by the fire. She looked at Philip Wakem. 'He is a kind boy,' she thought. 'But he is sad.'

And Philip looked at Maggie. 'She has beautiful dark eyes,' he thought. 'She is a kind and gentle girl.'

At last, Tom closed his book.

'Come upstairs with me, Maggie,' he said. 'I've got a secret!'

21

Tom was not dead. But his foot was badly hurt. Tom had to stay in bed. Maggie took care of him. She stayed at the school for a week.

One afternoon, Tom was asleep. Maggie and Philip were sitting in the library.

'Maggie, I do not have a sister,' Philip said quietly. 'Will you be my sister? I love you, Maggie.'

'I love my brother,' Maggie replied. 'But I love you too, Philip. I am going away to school soon. I will not see you again.'

'I will never forget you, Maggie,' Philip said. 'I will never forget your beautiful dark eyes.'

'Thank you,' said Maggie. And she kissed Philip quickly.

5

Mr Tulliver Loses Everything

In 1833, Tom Tulliver was sixteen. Philip Wakem had left Mr Stelling's school. Tom was still studying at the school.

It was a cold November day. Tom was alone in the school library. The door opened and Maggie came into the room. She was as tall as Tom and she was very beautiful.

'Maggie!' Tom said. 'Why are you here? Why are you not at your school?'

'Oh, Tom! Something terrible has happened,' said Maggie.

'What is it? Tell me, Maggie!' Tom said.

'Father has lost the law suit, Tom,' said Maggie. 'Father must pay for everything. He must pay our neighbour's lawyer – Mr Wakem.'

'Lost the law suit! Father must pay Wakem money!' Tom shouted.

Maggie started to cry. 'There is more bad news, Tom,' she said. 'Father has no money. He cannot pay Wakem. He will lose the mill, his land, everything. Mother cries all the time. And Father—'

'Is Father ill?' Tom asked.

'Father is very ill,' Maggie replied. 'He cannot walk. He has forgotten everything. Tom, you must come back to the mill!'

'I hate Wakem and I hate his son,' Tom said angrily. 'Never speak to Philip Wakem again, Maggie!'

———

Tom and Maggie went back to Dorlcote Mill. Mrs Tulliver was waiting for them.

'Oh, Tom!' she said. 'Wakem's men will take our furniture, our clothes, everything!'

The next day, Mr and Mrs Glegg came to the mill. Mrs Deane was with them.

'How is Mr Tulliver?' Mr Glegg asked.

'He has forgotten everything,' Mrs Tulliver replied. 'And he has lost everything. We have no money. We have nothing!'

'This is terrible news,' said Mrs Deane.

'There is no money to pay for education,' said Mrs Glegg. 'Tom must get a job. And Maggie must stay here. She must help her mother.'

Tom spoke to his aunts. 'Please lend me some money,' he said. 'I will get a job. I will pay the money back to you.'

'Your aunts cannot lend you any money,' said Mr Glegg. 'They need their money. They get interest on their money.'

———

The next day, Tom went to his Uncle Deane's office. Mr Deane worked for Guest and Company in St Ogg's.

'Uncle, please give me a job,' Tom said.

'How old are you, Tom?' Mr Deane asked.

'Sixteen – nearly seventeen,' Tom replied.

'You had a good education,' said Mr Deane. 'But Latin will not help you here.'

'I can learn other things,' said Tom.

'I will give you a job in the office,' said Mr Deane. 'But you must work hard.'

'Thank you, Uncle,' Tom said. He shook hands with his uncle and he left the office.

Outside the office, he saw a notice on the wall.

TO BE SOLD

Dorlcote Mill

with house, land and furniture

Mr Tulliver was very ill. He stayed in his bed for two months. On a cold day in January, he came into the dining-room.

'Where is the furniture?' Mr Tulliver asked.

'Wakem's men took it,' Maggie said. 'They sold it. But here is your chair. Sit down, Father.'

'Then I have lost everything,' Mr Tulliver said.

'Yes, Father,' Tom replied. 'And we must pay Wakem three hundred pounds more. But I have a job. I will save my money. I will pay Wakem.'

'We will look after you, Father,' Maggie said.

Mrs Tulliver began to cry. 'Lawyer Wakem has bought the mill and the house,' she said.

'So we must leave the mill, Bessy,' Mr Tulliver replied sadly.

'No,' said Mrs Tulliver. 'You will work for Wakem. You will be the miller. We will stay here.'

At first, Mr Tulliver did not reply. Then he spoke.

'Tom, get the Bible!' he said.

'Yes, Father,' said Tom. He brought the Bible to his father.

'Write this,' said Mr Tulliver. ' "Edward Tulliver will work for Lawyer Wakem at Dorlcote Mill. But he will never forgive Wakem. He will always hate him." '

'Then write this, Tom,' said Mr Tulliver. ' "Tom Tulliver will never forgive Lawyer Wakem. He will always hate Wakem and his family." Then write your name.'

'Oh no, Tom,' said Maggie. 'Do not write that!'

'Be quiet, Maggie!' Tom said. 'I want to write it. I will write it.'

6

The Red Deeps

For a few years, the Tullivers' lives were difficult. Mr Tulliver hated Lawyer Wakem. But he had to work for the lawyer. Tom worked for Guest and Company, in St Ogg's. Tom saved all his money. Maggie stayed in the house. She helped her mother.

One day, in June 1837, Maggie's life changed.

That afternoon, she was very tired. 'I will walk to the Red Deeps,' she thought. 'I will be alone there.'

The Red Deeps was a beautiful, quiet place. There were many tall trees there. The grass was soft, and the earth on the ground was red. Maggie liked the Red Deeps.

Maggie walked slowly under the trees. But she was not alone. Philip Wakem was in the Red Deeps too.

Maggie had not seen Philip for five years.

'Philip! Why are you here?' Maggie asked.

'I saw you leaving Dorlcote Mill,' Philip replied. 'I followed you. I have never forgotten you, Maggie. You are beautiful.'

'Am I beautiful, Philip?' Maggie said. 'I am not beautiful. I am very unhappy.'

'I am unhappy too, Maggie,' Philip said. 'I am a man now. But I will never be tall and strong. My back will always be twisted.'

'Oh, Philip, that is not important,' Maggie said.

'Will we meet again?' Philip asked. 'Will you be my friend?'

'No, Philip,' Maggie said. 'We must not meet again. We must not be friends. I must go now. Goodbye.'

And Maggie walked away quickly.

'I will come here again,' Philip thought. 'I want to meet Maggie. I want to be her friend.'

Philip walked to the Red Deeps every day. Then one afternoon, he saw Maggie again. They talked for a long time. After that, they often met in the Red Deeps. But Maggie told nobody. Their meetings were secret.

One day, Philip said, 'I love you Maggie. I want to marry you.'

'We cannot get married,' Maggie replied. 'The Tullivers hate the Wakems. I love you but I cannot marry you.'

A year passed. One day, Tom saw Philip Wakem walking from the Red Deeps. Tom went back to the house. Maggie was reading a book. Tom looked at Maggie's shoes. There was red earth on them.

'Maggie, have you been to the Red Deeps?' Tom asked.

Maggie looked at her shoes. She saw the red earth. It was earth from the ground at the Red Deeps.

'Yes, I have been there,' she said. 'I went for a walk.'

'Did you meet Philip Wakem there?' Tom asked.

'Yes, Tom,' Maggie replied. 'I often meet him there. We talk about books and music. He lends me books.'

Tom was angry. 'Father hates Lawyer Wakem. And I hate him too,' Tom said. 'You must not talk to his son!'

'Philip loves me,' Maggie replied. 'And I love him.'

'You are a bad daughter and a bad sister!' Tom said.

The next afternoon, Tom went with Maggie to the Red Deeps. Philip Wakem was there. He was waiting for Maggie. Philip looked at Tom. Then he looked at Maggie and he understood everything. Tom spoke first.

'You and Maggie have met secretly,' he said. 'She is a bad sister! And you are a bad man! Your body is twisted and your mind is twisted too!'

Tom went towards Philip and he lifted his hand. 'Don't write to Maggie!' he said. 'Don't speak to her! I'll beat you—'

'Tom, please stop!' said Maggie. She was crying. 'Forgive me, Philip,' she said.

'I understand, Maggie,' said Philip. 'You have an unkind, stupid brother. I love you, Maggie. Tom does not love you.'

Tom pulled Maggie's arm. 'Come home, Maggie,' he said angrily.

Maggie touched Philip's hand. Then Philip turned away. Tom and Maggie walked back to the mill.

'Tom, you were cruel to Philip,' Maggie said. 'You are very hard, Tom. You are very unkind.'

7

Edward Tulliver Dies

Three weeks passed. Tom did not speak to Maggie. One afternoon, he came back to the house at two o'clock. He spoke to his father.

'I have good news, Father,' Tom said. 'Uncle Deane lent me some money. I have traded with the money. I have bought goods and sold them well. I have three hundred and twenty pounds. We can pay Lawyer Wakem.'

'Bessy,' said Mr Tulliver, 'we have a good son.'

The next afternoon, Mr Tulliver went to St Ogg's with Tom. They rode their horses to Lawyer Wakem's office. The lawyer was not there but they left three hundred pounds for him. Then Tom went to the office of Guest and Company. Mr Tulliver rode back to the mill.

A man on a horse was waiting outside the mill. It was Lawyer Wakem.

'I want to speak to you, Tulliver,' said Wakem.

'I will speak first,' Mr Tulliver shouted. 'I have left three hundred pounds at your office. I have paid you all your money. I will not work for you now!'

'Good! I don't want you,' Wakem replied. 'You are a very stupid man, Tulliver!'

'And you are a very bad man!' Tulliver shouted.

'I am going!' Wakem said. 'Move your horse!'

Mr Tulliver lifted his riding <u>whip</u>. He rode towards the lawyer. Wakem's horse was frightened. It turned suddenly and Wakem fell to the ground. Mr Tulliver got off his horse. He started to beat the lawyer with his riding whip.

'Help! Help!' Wakem shouted.

Maggie and Mrs Tulliver ran out of the house. Maggie screamed.

'Stop, Father, stop!' she shouted. She held her father's arms. 'Please stop, Father,' she said. 'Mother, help Mr Wakem!'

Wakem stood up. He got onto his horse.

'I will not forget this, Tulliver!' he said. And he rode slowly away.

'Father, come into the house,' said Maggie.

Mr Tulliver did not move. 'I am ill,' he said. 'Help me. There is a pain in my head.'

Maggie and her mother took Mr Tulliver into the house.

'Go and get Tom,' Mr Tulliver said.

Maggie ran to St Ogg's. She went to Guest and Company's office. 'Come quickly, Tom,' she said.

———

Mr Tulliver lay in bed. He could not move. He was very ill. Tom, Maggie and Mrs Tulliver sat by the bed.

'What shall I do, Father?' asked Tom.

'Save your money. Buy the mill from Wakem,' Mr Tulliver said.

'Yes, Father,' said Tom.

'Take care of your mother. And take care of your sister,' Mr Tulliver said.

'Yes, Father, I will,' said Tom.

'Kiss me, Maggie,' said Mr Tulliver. 'Kiss me, Bessy. Goodbye, my son.' And he died.

Tom and Maggie looked at each other.

'We must always love each other, Tom,' Maggie said.

Tom held his sister's hand.

'Yes, Maggie,' he said.

8

Stephen Guest

The Tulliver family left Dorlcote Mill. Tom lived alone in St Ogg's. He worked hard.

Mrs Tulliver went to St Ogg's too. Mrs Deane had died. Mrs Tulliver lived with Lucy and Mr Deane. Maggie went away. She became a teacher in a school.

Two years passed. It was an afternoon in April 1840. Maggie was back in St Ogg's for a holiday. She was talking to Lucy Deane.

'I hate teaching,' said Maggie.

'You must stay here, Maggie,' Lucy said. 'Aunt Tulliver will look after us all. Don't go back to the school.'

'Thank you,' Maggie said. 'I will be happy here.'

Maggie looked out of the open window. The Deanes' house was next to the River Floss. 'The river is very beautiful,' Maggie said. 'And you are beautiful too. Are you happy, Lucy? Do you have many friends? Are you in love?'

Lucy looked down at her hands. 'Yes,' she said. 'I am in love with Stephen Guest.'

Maggie smiled. 'Tell me about him, Lucy,' she said.

'Stephen is clever and handsome,' said Lucy. 'He loves me and I love him. He likes music. His friend, Philip Wakem, likes music too. We will sing together!'

'Oh, Lucy, I must not meet Philip Wakem,' Maggie

said. 'Tom hates him. Philip and I were in love. But my father hated Mr Wakem. And Tom hates Philip.'

'That is a sad story,' Lucy said. 'I will make you happy. Philip is in Italy now. But he will come back soon. I will speak to Tom. Tom and Philip must be friends.'

'You will marry Philip,' said Lucy. 'And I will marry Stephen. We shall all be happy!'

A few moments later, a tall young man came into the room.

Stephen bowed. He looked at Maggie. She was very beautiful!

The next day, Maggie went to St Ogg's. She saw her brother, Tom. He lived alone in St Ogg's.

'Hello, Maggie,' said Tom. 'Are you well?'

'Yes, I am well, Tom,' Maggie replied. 'I am not going back to the school. I am going to live with Mother at the Deanes' house.'

'Tom,' Maggie said, 'I must tell you something. Philip Wakem is coming back to St Ogg's. Philip is Lucy's friend. He will come to her house. I shall meet him there.'

'I hate Philip Wakem,' said Tom.

'Oh, Tom,' Maggie said, 'Lucy is my friend. And she is Philip's friend. I want to speak to Philip.'

'Yes, Maggie,' Tom replied, 'I understand. And I want to be a good brother. Speak to Philip, Maggie. But you must not meet him alone.'

'And I want to be a good sister,' said Maggie. 'Thank you, Tom.'

9

Happy Days

Maggie was happy at the Deanes' house. Stephen often came to see Lucy. The three young people sometimes went in a boat on the River Floss. In the evenings, they sang together. Maggie, Lucy and Stephen laughed. They were happy. But Maggie and Stephen were starting to love each other.

One evening in May, Maggie was sitting in the garden. She was reading a book. She heard a sound and she looked towards the river. Stephen was getting out of a boat. He walked towards her.

'Good evening, Miss Tulliver,' said Stephen. He held up some papers. 'I have brought these songs for Lucy,' he said.

'Lucy is not here,' Maggie said. 'We will not sing tonight.'

'Philip Wakem has come to St Ogg's,' Stephen said. 'I saw him this morning. He will come here tomorrow.'

Maggie's book fell to the ground. Stephen quickly picked it up. He gave the book to Maggie. Stephen's fingers touched Maggie's fingers. They looked at each other.

'I must go,' Stephen said.

'Please stay,' said Maggie.

'No, Maggie. Will you give Lucy the songs?'

'Yes.'

'And Philip will come here tomorrow. Will you tell Lucy?'

'Yes.'

Stephen walked away. He got into his boat.

'Oh, why did Maggie come to St Ogg's?' Stephen thought. 'I love her. I must not meet her alone.'

———

The next morning, Philip Wakem came to the Deanes' house. Maggie was alone. She said, 'I have spoken to Tom. We shall be friends, Philip.' And she smiled at him.

A few minutes later, Lucy and Stephen came into the room.

'Sing your new song, Stephen,' Lucy said. 'Will you play the piano, Philip?'

Philip played the piano and Stephen sang his song. Maggie was very happy. Her face was beautiful. She looked at Stephen and he looked at her. Philip looked at Maggie too. He understood everything.

10

'I Love You'

Stephen Guest and his family lived at Park House, near St Ogg's. At the end of May, there was a dance at Park House. There were bright lights in the rooms. There was music. People were dancing.

Stephen Guest was dancing with Lucy. She was very happy. Maggie was happy too. She loved music and dancing.

At first, Stephen did not speak to Maggie. But he looked at her many times. He wanted to dance with

her. He wanted to hold her hand. But he danced with Lucy.

Then Stephen saw Maggie again. She was sitting alone. He went towards her. Maggie looked at him and she smiled.

'It is very warm here,' Stephen said. 'Shall we go into the garden?'

Maggie stood up. Stephen held her arm. They walked together into the garden. They stood near some red roses. Maggie held one of the flowers. It had a sweet smell.

'The flowers are very beautiful,' said Maggie. Stephen did not answer.

Suddenly, Stephen touched Maggie's arm. Then he kissed it, again and again.

Maggie pulled her arm away. Her dark eyes were angry.

'Stephen!' she said. 'This is wrong! You love Lucy! Please go away now. We must never meet alone again!'

Maggie went quickly into the house. A few minutes later, Stephen followed her.

Maggie listened to the music. She talked to people. She smiled. But she did not look at Stephen Guest.

———

A few days later, Maggie was walking by the river. She was alone. She heard a sound behind her and she turned round.

Stephen Guest was riding towards her. Stephen got off his horse.

'Please walk with me, Maggie,' Stephen said. 'I must talk to you.'

'Why are you here?' Maggie said. 'We must not meet alone.'

'You are angry,' Stephen said. 'I understand. But I love you. I love you, Maggie.'

'You must not say that,' Maggie said. 'You must go away, Stephen.'

'I love you. Please love me,' Stephen replied.

'Don't say that!' Maggie said. 'You love Lucy, Stephen.'

'Do you love me, Maggie?' Stephen asked. 'Tell me, Maggie!'

Maggie did not answer. She started to cry.

'We love each other,' Stephen said. 'Lucy will understand.'

'I love you, Stephen,' Maggie said. 'But I love Lucy too. She is my friend. I cannot be cruel to Lucy. Please, Stephen, leave me. Please, go away.'

Stephen looked at Maggie. There were tears in her beautiful, dark eyes.

'I will go,' Stephen said. 'Kiss me, and I will go.'

Maggie kissed him. 'Please, go now,' she said. Stephen got onto his horse and he rode away.

11

The River Floss

One day in early June, Maggie and Lucy were talking.

'Maggie, I have some good news,' Lucy said. 'My father and Mr Guest are going to buy Dorlcote Mill. Tom will be the miller. Aunt Tulliver will live at the mill with Tom.'

'And Philip has told his father about you, Maggie,' Lucy said. 'Mr Wakem wants to meet you. You and Philip will get married!'

'I am happy about the mill,' Maggie said. 'But I will not marry Philip. I am going to leave St Ogg's at the end of June.'

'Leave St Ogg's?' said Lucy. 'Why, Maggie?'

'I must work. I must get a job,' Maggie replied.

———

So Tom and Mrs Tulliver went to live at Dorlcote Mill again. Stephen came to the Deanes' house every day. Philip was often there too.

In the evenings, the four young people often sang together. Stephen sang love songs. He did not sing them for Lucy. He sang them for Maggie. But Lucy did not understand.

One evening in late June, Lucy said, 'Let's go in the boat tomorrow. We will go down the river. We will go to Luckreth.'

'Four people in the boat is too many,' Stephen said.

'Philip, you go tomorrow with Lucy and Maggie. I will go with them the next day.'

'Then Maggie and I will meet you tomorrow, Philip,' Lucy said. 'Come at half-past ten.'

But the next morning, Lucy had to go with her father to another town. At half-past ten, Stephen Guest came into the house. Maggie was alone.

'Where is Philip?' Maggie asked.

'He is ill. He cannot come,' Stephen replied. 'Where is Lucy?'

'Lucy is not here,' Maggie said. 'She is with her father. We cannot go without her.'

'Please come, Maggie,' Stephen said. 'You are going away soon. I will not see you again. Let's go on the river for an hour.'

'I will come with you for an hour, Stephen,' Maggie replied. 'After that, we must not be alone again.'

They walked down to the river and got into the boat. The sun was shining. Stephen rowed the boat and it moved quickly over the water.

'Lucy will come back this afternoon,' said Maggie. 'We must come back before two o'clock.'

The sun was hot. Stephen stopped rowing. The water carried the boat along. Stephen and Maggie were very happy. They did not think about the time.

But much later, Maggie cried out, 'We have passed Luckreth! Where are we? It is very late. What will Lucy say? We must go back!'

Stephen held Maggie's hand. She was crying.

'Let's not go back! Let's get married!' Stephen said.

Maggie did not answer. She could not speak. She could not think.

'We must get married, Maggie!' Stephen said. 'We are together now – forever.'

Stephen started rowing again. He did not turn the boat round. The river was wide. The water rushed past. There were no villages next to the river.

Suddenly, Stephen saw a steamboat.

'Look, Maggie,' he said. 'The steamboat is going to Mudport. We will get onto the steamboat. We will get married in Mudport!'

Maggie was very unhappy.

Stephen and Maggie got onto the steamboat. Stephen spoke to the captain of the steamboat.

'This lady – my wife – is very tired,' Stephen said. 'Please take us to Mudport. I will pay you well.'

Maggie sat down and she went to sleep. Night came. All night, Stephen sat next to Maggie.

12

'I Cannot Marry You'

Maggie woke very early in the morning. She remembered everything. She was on a steamboat. She was with Stephen. She started to cry.

'Don't cry, Maggie,' Stephen said. 'We will be in Mudport this afternoon. We will get married.'

But Maggie did not speak. She was too unhappy.

They got off the steamboat at Mudport. Stephen took Maggie to an inn.

'I will not marry you, Stephen,' Maggie said. 'You must leave me now.'

'I cannot live without you, Maggie,' Stephen said. 'I cannot go now.'

'Then I will go,' said Maggie. 'Yesterday, I could not leave you. Today, I can leave you. Goodbye, Stephen.'

'Maggie!' Stephen said. 'I was wrong yesterday. I'm sorry!'

'We were both wrong yesterday,' Maggie said.

'But we love each other,' Stephen said. 'That cannot be wrong.'

'We are being cruel to Lucy,' said Maggie. 'That is wrong! I love you, but I cannot marry you. I am going back to St Ogg's – alone!'

'No!' Stephen shouted. 'People will say, "Maggie is a bad woman." Your life will be terrible!'

'I will tell Lucy everything,' Maggie said. 'She will

understand. She will forgive me. And she will forgive you, Stephen.'

Stephen said nothing. Maggie left the inn. She went back to St Ogg's.

13

Three Letters

Tom Tulliver and his mother were at Dorlcote Mill. Tom was standing outside the house. He looked down at the river. The water was rushing past. Then Tom turned towards the house. He was angry.

Maggie was standing by the door. She was very unhappy.

'Tom, I have come back,' Maggie said.

'You are a bad woman,' Tom said. 'I don't want you here.'

Mrs Tulliver came to the door of the house. She listened.

'I was wrong, Tom,' Maggie said. 'I am sorry.'

'I don't believe you,' Tom replied. 'Lucy was your friend. Now she is ill and unhappy. I will give you some money. But you cannot live here!'

Maggie started to cry. Mrs Tulliver came out of the house. She went to Maggie and she kissed her.

'I'll go with you, my child,' Mrs Tulliver said.

———

Maggie and her mother went to St Ogg's. They lived in a small house next to the river. But Maggie wanted to live alone. After a few days, Mrs Tulliver went back to the mill.

Stephen Guest went away. He wrote a letter to his father.

Father ~

I was wrong. I loved Maggie Tulliver and I wanted to marry her. Maggie is good. She is not a bad woman. Please show this letter to Lucy. Ask her to forgive me.

Stephen

At the beginning of July, Maggie got a letter from Philip.

Maggie,

You are good. You are strong. I met you ten years ago. I loved you and you loved me. I love you now, Maggie. I shall always be your friend.

Yours ever, Philip Wakem

Three weeks later, Maggie was sitting in the house next to the river. She was sitting by a window. She was looking at the River Floss. Suddenly, someone spoke her name. She turned round.

'Lucy!' said Maggie.

Lucy went to her cousin and kissed her.

'I am happy to see you, Lucy,' Maggie said. 'I am sorry about Stephen.'

'I understand,' Lucy said. 'You loved him and you sent him away. That was good. You were strong.'

'Forgive him, Lucy,' Maggie said. 'He will come back.'

'I have been ill,' Lucy said. 'I am going away. But I will come back soon and I will visit you again.'

Maggie kissed her cousin.

'Goodbye, Maggie,' Lucy said quietly.

———

In August, the weather was very bad. The rain fell.
Hour after hour, it rained. Day after day, it rained. Was
there going to be a flood? The water in the River Floss
was rising higher and higher.

One day, Maggie got a letter from Stephen.

My dearest Maggie –
Why did you leave me? Maggie, you
took away your love. You took
away my life! Maggie, I want
to be with you.

I am yours forever –   Stephen

Maggie was lonely and unhappy. She sat in the little
house next to the River Floss. She read Stephen's letter many times. She cried and cried.

Hours passed. Night came. The rain fell all night.
The river rose higher and higher.

14

The Flood

Suddenly, Maggie was very cold. She looked down. The floor was covered with water! The River Floss had flooded!

Maggie was in great danger. Her house was next to the river. And there was water in the house!

Maggie ran to a window and she opened it. She looked outside. It was dark. But she could see water everywhere. The streets of St Ogg's were covered with rushing water.

There was a little boat outside the house. It was tied to the wall. Maggie climbed through a window and she got into the boat. She untied the boat. The water carried the boat away from the house. Maggie was alone in the darkness!

The boat moved very fast. The flooded river was carrying it along. Maggie was very frightened.

———

The rushing river carried the boat out of the town. Maggie saw the tops of trees and the tops of buildings.

'I must go to the mill,' she thought. 'I must help Tom and Mother.'

Maggie started to row. The boat left the river. Soon Maggie's boat was moving over the flooded fields.

At last Maggie saw Dorlcote Mill.

'Tom! Where are you?' Maggie shouted. 'Mother! This is Maggie!'

Tom was in the house. He was upstairs. He looked out of a window.

'You have come, Maggie,' he said.

'Yes, Tom,' Maggie replied. 'Where is Mother?'

'Mother is not here. But she is safe,' Tom said.

Tom got into the boat. 'I will row, Maggie,' he said.

Tom sat down in front of Maggie.

'We must go to Park House,' said Maggie. 'It's on higher ground.'

Tom started to row. He looked at Maggie. Brother and sister were together again.

———

The sun was rising. Tom rowed on. Soon they were on the River Floss again. Maggie looked behind Tom. There were great trees in the rushing water. The trees were coming towards them. Maggie screamed.

'Tom! Look behind you!' she shouted.

Tom turned round. He saw the danger. But he could do nothing. He held his sister in his arms.

'We are going to die, Maggie,' he said.

A great tree hit the boat. The boat went under the water. Soon the boat came up again – but it was empty.

———

Days later, some people found Tom and Maggie. They were in each other's arms. They were dead.

Heinemann English Language Teaching
A division of Reed Educational and Professional Publishing Limited
Halley Court, Jordan Hill, Oxford OX2 8EJ

OXFORD MADRID FLORENCE ATHENS PRAGUE
SÃO PAULO MEXICO CITY CHICAGO PORTSMOUTH (NH)
TOKYO SINGAPORE KUALA LUMPUR MELBOURNE
AUCKLAND JOHANNESBURG IBADAN GABORONE

ISBN 0 435 27337 X

This retold version for Heinemann Guided Readers
Text © Florence Bell 1997
Design and illustration © Reed Educational and
Professional Publishing Limited 1997
First published 1997

Acknowledgement: The publishers would like to thank Popperfoto
for permission to reproduce the picture on page 4.

Illustrated by Shirley Bellwood. Map on page 3, by John Gilkes
Typography by Adrian Hodgkins
Designed by Sue Vaudin
Cover by Sarah Perkins and Marketplace Design
Typeset in 12/16 Goudy
Printed and bound in Malta by Interprint Limited

97 98 99 00 10 9 8 7 6 5 4 3 2 1